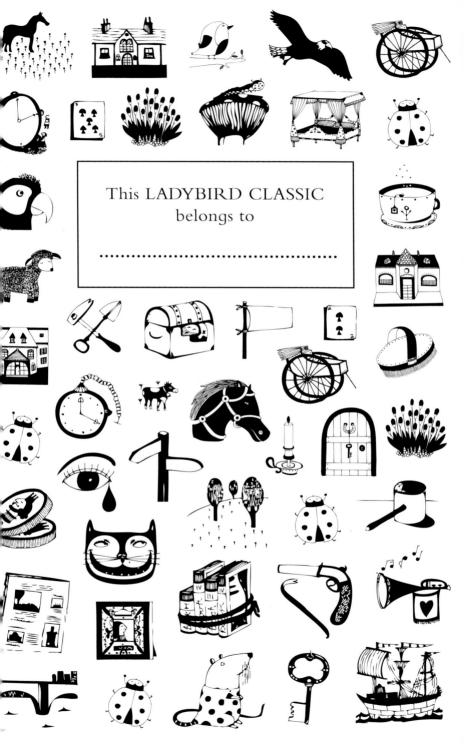

This LADYBIRD CLASSIC
belongs to

....

A History of the Author

Lewis Carroll is the pseudonym of
Charles Lutwidge Dodgson, who was born
in 1832 and was a lecturer in mathematics
at Christ Church College, Oxford.
Alice in Wonderland and its sequel, *Through the
Looking-Glass*, began as stories Dodgson made
up for Alice Liddell, the daughter of friends.

Chapter illustrations by Valeria Valenza

Marks and Spencer plc
PO Box 3339
Chester CH99 9QS

shop online
www.marksandspencer.com

ISBN 978-0-241-25342-7
Printed in China

LADYBIRD 🐞 CLASSICS

Alice in Wonderland

by Lewis Carroll

Retold by Joan Collins
Illustrated by Ester García-Cortés

M&S
KIDS

Contents

CHAPTER ONE

Down the Rabbit Hole

ALICE WAS TIRED of sitting by her sister on the grassy bank and having nothing to do. Her sister was reading a book with no pictures or conversations in it. It looked very dull.

It was a hot day, and Alice was sleepy. She was wondering whether to get up and make a daisy chain, when suddenly a white rabbit with pink eyes ran close by her.

'Oh dear! Oh dear! I shall be late!' the White Rabbit said. He took a watch out of his waistcoat pocket, looked at it and hurried on.

Alice had never seen a rabbit with a waistcoat before, nor one with a watch to take out of his pocket. She jumped to her feet and ran after him, just in time to see him pop down a large rabbit hole under the hedge. Alice followed him, never thinking how she was going to get out again.

The rabbit hole went on like a tunnel for some way, but suddenly Alice found herself falling down a very deep well. She was falling slowly, so she had time to look around and see all sorts of interesting things along the way.

'I wonder how many thousands of miles I've fallen?' she thought. 'I must be somewhere near the centre of the earth. Perhaps I'll fall right through to the other side!'

But just then, *thump, thump, thump*, down she came on a heap of leaves, without hurting herself at all. Ahead of her, at the end of a long passage, she saw the White Rabbit hurrying along. 'Oh, my ears and whiskers, how late it's getting!' she heard him say as he turned the corner.

Chapter Two

The Gold Key

BY THE TIME Alice reached the corner, the White Rabbit had gone. She found herself in a long hall lit by lamps in the ceiling. There were doors all the way round, but they were locked. How was she going to get out?

She then saw a little table made of glass. On top of it was a gold key. But it was too small to unlock any of the doors.

Then Alice noticed a low curtain. Behind it she found a tiny door, only fifteen inches high. The key fitted perfectly!

Alice had to kneel down to look through the door. There was a small passage, not much larger than a rat hole, that led to the loveliest garden she had ever seen. But she was too big to get her head through the doorway.

'I wish I could shut up like a telescope!' she said to herself.

She walked back to the glass table. To her surprise there was a bottle on it, which had not been there before. A label round its neck said 'DRINK ME' in large letters.

Alice took a sip. It was delicious and tasted of all Alice's favourite foods. So she drank it up.

'What a curious feeling!' said Alice. 'I *must* be shutting up like a telescope!' And so she was! Soon she was only ten inches

DRINK ME

high, just the right size to go through the little door into the lovely garden.

But poor Alice! When she got to the door, she realized that she had left the gold key on top of the glass table, and now she was too small to reach it. She tried to climb up one of the table legs, but it was too slippery. At last, tired out, she sat down and cried.

Then she noticed a little glass box on the floor, just under the table. Inside it was a very small cake with the words 'EAT ME' beautifully marked on it in currants.

'Well, I'll eat it,' thought Alice. 'If it makes me larger I can reach the key, and if it makes me smaller I can creep under the door. So either way I'll get into the garden.'

She nibbled the cake, and soon she had finished it all up.

CHAPTER THREE

The Pool of Tears

'CURIOUSER AND CURIOUSER!'
cried Alice. 'Now I'm opening out like the
largest telescope that ever was!'

Her feet were so far away that she
wondered how she would get her shoes and
stockings off and on. Then her head struck
against the ceiling. Alice was more than
nine feet tall!

She picked up the little gold key and

hurried off to the garden door. But poor Alice could only look into the garden with one eye by lying down on the floor. She sat down and began to cry again.

'What a great baby you are!' she scolded herself, but she could not stop crying. Soon there was a large pool of tears around her, reaching halfway down the hall.

After a while, she heard a pattering of feet in the distance. Alice dried her eyes and saw the White Rabbit coming back. He was carrying a fan and a pair of white gloves and muttering, 'Oh, the Duchess! Oh, the Duchess! Won't she be cross if I've kept her waiting!'

'Please, sir, could you help me?' asked Alice timidly. But when he saw her the White Rabbit dropped his fan and gloves and scurried off as quickly as he could.

Alice picked up the things he had dropped. It was very hot, so she began to

fan herself. She felt very strange.

'I'm not at all my usual self!' she thought. 'Perhaps I've changed into somebody else! I'll see if I still know the things I learned at school: four times five is twelve, and five times six is thirteen … London is the capital of Paris, and Paris is the capital of Rome… That can't be right!' she sobbed. 'I must be somebody else!'

Then she noticed that she had managed to put on one of the White Rabbit's little gloves. 'I'm small again!' she cried, and ran off to the garden door. But now it was shut, and the gold key was back on the glass table.

'Now things are worse than ever!' she thought. Her foot slipped, and *splash!* she was up to her chin in salt water, in the pool of tears.

CHAPTER FOUR

The Mouse's Tale

ALICE SOON FOUND that she was
not alone: a mouse was swimming a little
way off. To Alice it looked as big as a
hippopotamus.

'Oh, Mouse,' she said politely, 'do
you know the way out of this pool?'
The Mouse did not answer.

'Perhaps it's a French mouse and doesn't
speak English,' thought Alice. She only

knew one sentence in French from school. 'Où est mon chat?' she asked hopefully.

The Mouse nearly jumped out of the water and quivered with fright.

'Oh, I beg your pardon!' apologized Alice. 'I forgot mice don't like cats!'

'Would you like cats – or dogs – if you were me?' squeaked the Mouse indignantly.

'I suppose not!' said Alice, and they swam together to the shore.

A strange, bedraggled collection of birds and animals had gathered there. They were running races in circles, organized by a dodo, to get themselves dry, and Alice and the Mouse watched them with interest.

When the races were finished, Alice asked the Mouse to tell her about himself and why he hated 'C and D'. (She was afraid to say 'cats and dogs'!)

'Mine is a long and sad tale,' he said, sighing.

Alice had been looking at the Mouse's tail as he spoke. 'It is long,' she said, 'but why do you call it sad?' So when he began his story, Alice's idea of it was something like this:

'Fury said to a mouse,
that he met in the house,
"Let us both go to law: *I* will
prosecute *you*. Come,
I'll take no denial,
we must have the
trial, for really this
morning I've nothing
to do." Said the
mouse to the
cur, "Such a
trial, dear Sir,
with no jury
or judge, would
be wasting
our breath."
"I'll be judge,
I'll be jury,"
said cunning
old Fury.
"I'll try
the whole
cause
and
condemn
you
to
death."'

'You're not attending,' the Mouse said crossly.

'Yes, I am!' said Alice. 'I think you'd got to the fifth bend.'

'I had NOT!' said the Mouse sharply.

'A knot?' said Alice, always ready to help. 'Oh, let me help you to undo it!' But the Mouse was offended and would not stay to finish his story.

CHAPTER FIVE

Advice from a Caterpillar

MEANWHILE, THE WHITE Rabbit's fan and gloves had vanished, and so had the pool of tears, the hall and the glass table. Instead, Alice found herself on the edge of a wood.

She ran through grass and flowers till she came to a mushroom that was as big as she was. On top of it sat a large, blue caterpillar with its arms folded, quietly smoking a hookah, which is a sort of long, curly water pipe.

At first the Caterpillar took no notice of Alice. But after a while it took the hookah out of its mouth and asked in a sleepy voice, 'Who are you?'

Poor Alice was not at all sure who she was.

'I can't remember things as I used to, and I don't stay the same size for ten minutes together,' she said.

'What size do you want to be?' asked the Caterpillar.

'I'm not really particular about size,' replied Alice. 'But I should like to be a little larger than I am now! Three inches is such a silly size to be!'

The Caterpillar drew itself up to its full height, which was exactly three inches tall! 'It is a very good height indeed!' it said angrily, and began to crawl away.

As it went, the Caterpillar remarked,

'One side will make you taller, and the other side will make you shorter.'

'One side of what?' asked Alice.

'Of the mushroom, of course!' said the Caterpillar crossly, and a moment later it was out of sight.

Alice put her arms round the edges of the mushroom, as far as she could reach, and broke off two pieces. She nibbled each piece in turn till she had managed to bring her height up to just nine inches. Then she set off again till she came to a house.

Alice went up to the door and knocked timidly. There was a most extraordinary noise going on inside – howling, sneezing, and every so often a crash as if a dish had been broken. There was no answer to her knock, so Alice pushed the door open and marched in.

Chapter Six

Pig and Pepper

THE DOOR LED into a large kitchen
full of smoke. A duchess was sitting on
a three-legged stool in the middle of
the room, nursing a baby. The cook was
leaning over the fire, stirring an iron pot
full of soup and shaking a pepper-pot
into it.

The air was thick with pepper. The
Duchess was sneezing, and the baby was

howling and sneezing in turns. A large cat was lying on the hearth rug, grinning from ear to ear.

'Why does your cat grin like that?' asked Alice.

'It's a Cheshire Cat!' said the Duchess. 'Pig!'

Alice, startled, thought the Duchess was addressing her. But it was the baby she meant.

Suddenly the cook took the pot off the fire and began throwing soup over everything within reach. When it was all gone, she threw the poker and tongs, saucepans, dishes and plates at the Duchess and the baby.

'Oh, mind what you're doing!' cried Alice, as a large saucepan lid whizzed past the baby's nose.

The Duchess took no notice and began to sing a lullaby to the baby. She threw it up and down, giving it a violent shake at

the end of each line.

'Speak roughly to your little boy,
And beat him when he sneezes:
He only does it to annoy,
Because he knows it teases.'

CHORUS

(with which the cook and the baby joined in)

'Wow! Wow! Wow!'

'Here!' said the Duchess, flinging the baby at Alice. 'You may nurse it for a bit if you like. I must get ready to play croquet with the Queen.'

Alice could hardly hold the baby, it wriggled so. She took it outside and looked at its face. It had a turned-up nose and very small eyes. Suddenly it grunted. Alice looked at it in alarm. It had turned into a PIG!

She put it down quickly, and it trotted happily away into the wood.

'If it had grown up, it would have been

an ugly child,' thought Alice. 'But it makes quite a handsome pig!'

Next moment, Alice was surprised to see a Cheshire Cat sitting on the branch of a tree and grinning down at her.

'Does anyone else live near here?' Alice asked.

'In that direction,' said the Cat, waving its right paw, 'lives a hatter. And in that direction,' waving its other paw, 'lives a March Hare. Visit either: they're both mad. We're all mad here. I'm mad. You're mad.'

'How do you know I'm mad?' said Alice.

'You must be,' said the Cat, 'or you wouldn't have come here. Are you going to play croquet with the Queen today?'

'I haven't been invited yet,' said Alice.

'I'll be there!' said the Cat, and vanished.

Alice was still looking at the place where it had been, when it suddenly appeared again. 'What became of the baby?' it said. 'I forgot to ask.'

'It turned into a pig,' said Alice. 'I wish you wouldn't disappear so quickly! It makes me giddy!'

'All right,' said the Cat. And this time it vanished quite slowly, beginning with the end of its tail and ending with its grin, which remained for some time after the rest of it had gone.

'Well, I've often seen a cat without a grin,' said Alice. 'But I've never seen a grin without a cat before!'

CHAPTER SEVEN

The Mad Hatter's Tea Party

ALICE EASILY RECOGNIZED the
March Hare's house. The chimneys were
shaped like ears, and the roof was covered
with fur.

At a table in front of the house, the
March Hare and the Hatter were having
tea. A dormouse was sitting between them.
It was asleep, and the other two were
using it as a cushion, resting their elbows

on it and talking over its head.

The table was a large one, but all three were crowded together at one corner of it. 'No room! No room!' they cried, when they saw Alice coming.

'There's plenty of room,' said Alice indignantly, sitting down in a large armchair.

'Have some wine!' said the March Hare.

'I don't see any wine,' said Alice, looking round.

'There isn't any!' said the March Hare.

'It wasn't very polite of you to offer it, then!' said Alice angrily.

'It wasn't very polite of you to sit down without being asked!' said the March Hare.

Then the Hatter joined in. 'Why is a raven like a writing desk?' he asked Alice.

'I believe I can guess that...' began Alice.

'Do you mean you think you can find

out the answer?' asked the March Hare.

'Exactly so,' said Alice.

'Then you should say what you mean,' said the March Hare.

'I do,' Alice replied. 'At least, I mean what I say, and that's the same thing, you know!'

'Not the same thing at all!' said the Hatter. 'You might as well say that "I see what I eat" is the same thing as "I eat what I see"!'

'You might as well say,' added the March Hare, 'that "I like what I get" is the same thing as "I get what I like"!'

While Alice thought about how to reply to this, the Mad Hatter took out his watch and looked at it. He shook it every now and then and held it to his ear.

'Two days wrong!' he said. 'I told you butter wouldn't suit the works!' He looked angrily at the March Hare.

'It was the best butter!' said the March Hare.

'Yes, but some crumbs must have got in as well,' the Hatter grumbled. 'You shouldn't have put it in with a bread knife!'

The March Hare took the watch and looked at it gloomily. Then he dipped it in his cup of tea and looked at it again. 'Let's change the subject,' he said. 'I vote the young lady tells us a story.'

'But I don't know one!' said Alice in alarm.

'Then the Dormouse shall!' they both cried. 'Wake up, Dormouse!' They pinched it on both sides at once, and the Hatter poured a little hot tea on its nose.

'I wasn't asleep!' murmured the Dormouse. 'I heard every word you said!'

'Tell us a story!' said the March Hare.

'Yes, please do,' said Alice.

'Once upon a time there were three sisters,' began the Dormouse in a great hurry. 'Their names were Elsie, Lacie and

Tillie, and they lived at the bottom of a well.'

'What did they live on?' asked Alice.

'They lived on treacle,' said the Dormouse.

'They couldn't have,' said Alice. 'They'd have been ill!'

'So they were,' said the Dormouse. 'Very ill.'

'Have some more tea!' said the Hatter to Alice.

'I haven't had any yet,' said Alice, 'so how can I have any more?'

'You mean you can't have less!' said the Hatter. 'It's easy to have more than nothing!'

Alice turned back to the Dormouse. 'Why did they live at the bottom of a well?' she asked.

'It was a treacle well,' said the Dormouse. 'These sisters were learning to draw, you see.'

'What did they draw?' asked Alice.

'Treacle,' replied the Dormouse.

'I don't understand,' said Alice. 'Where did they draw the treacle from?'

'You can draw water from a water well,' said the Hatter, 'so why shouldn't you draw treacle from a treacle well?'

'But they were in the well!' cried Alice.

'Of course they were,' said the Dormouse. 'Well in!' He was getting sleepy again.

'They drew everything that begins with an M,' the Dormouse went on drowsily, 'such as Mousetraps and the Moon and Muchness. You say "Things are much of a Muchness" – did you ever see a drawing of a Muchness?'

'I don't think –' began Alice.

'Then you shouldn't talk!' snapped the Hatter.

This was too much for Alice. She got up and walked into the wood. When she looked back, she saw that the others were trying to put the Dormouse into the teapot.

CHAPTER EIGHT

The Queen's Croquet Ground

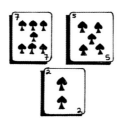

ALICE NOTICED A tree trunk in front of her with a door in it. She opened it and found herself back in the hall with the glass table and the gold key.

'This time I know what to do!' she said. She nibbled at the mushroom until she was small enough to go through the little door into the lovely garden with its flowerbeds and fountains.

Alice was surprised to see three gardeners busily painting a white rose tree red, and even more surprised when she saw that they were playing-cards. They were flat and oblong, with hands and feet at the corners. Their names were Two, Five and Seven.

'You see, miss, this here rose tree ought to have been red,' Two was explaining. 'If the Queen sees it, we shall all have our heads chopped off.'

'Hush!' whispered Five. 'Here she comes!' All three fell flat on their faces. There was a sound of many footsteps, and Alice looked round, eager to see the Queen.

First came ten soldiers, carrying clubs. Then came ten courtiers, decorated with diamonds. Then came the ten royal children, hand in hand, with hearts on their tunics. Next came the guests, including the Duchess and the White

Rabbit. And then came the Knave of Hearts, carrying a crown on a red velvet cushion. Last of all in the grand procession came the King and Queen of Hearts themselves.

Alice curtsied and told the Queen her name. 'I needn't be afraid of them!' she thought. 'They're only a pack of cards!'

The Queen looked at the gardeners, lying flat on the ground. 'Turn them over!' she said to the Knave.

The gardeners jumped up and started bowing to everyone. 'Off with their heads!' cried the Queen, and the procession moved off.

'You shan't be beheaded!' said Alice, popping the gardeners into a large flowerpot before the soldiers could catch them. Then she caught up with the procession.

'Get to your places!' shouted the Queen in a voice like thunder.

It was the strangest game of croquet Alice had ever seen. The balls were curled-up hedgehogs, and the mallets were flamingos. The soldiers had to double up and stand on their hands to make the arches. By the time Alice had her flamingo in position to tap the ball, her hedgehog had uncurled and crawled away.

The players didn't wait their turns and quarrelled over their hedgehogs. The Queen stamped about, shouting, 'Off with his head!' or, 'Off with her head!' every few minutes.

Soon the game was over. All the players, except the King and Queen and Alice, had been sentenced to be beheaded. Alice was relieved to hear the King whisper to them, 'You are all pardoned.'

Alice was talking to the Duchess when a trumpet sounded in the distance.

'The trial's beginning! Come on!' said the Duchess, taking Alice by the hand.

CHAPTER NINE

Who Stole the Tarts?

THE COURTROOM WAS crowded with small birds and animals, as well as the whole pack of cards. The King and Queen of Hearts were sitting on their thrones. The King, who was Judge, wore a wig with his crown on top of it.

Near the King stood the White Rabbit, with a trumpet in one hand and a parchment scroll in the other. The Knave of Hearts was in chains, standing between two soldiers.

On a table was a dish of tarts. (Alice hoped that they were the refreshments!)

There was a jury box with twelve creatures in it: animals, birds and a small lizard named Bill. They were all writing on slates. 'They're putting down their names, in case they forget them,' whispered the Duchess, digging her sharp little chin into Alice's shoulder.

'Stupid things!' said Alice in a loud voice.

'SILENCE IN COURT!' cried the White Rabbit. The jury were busy writing down 'Stupid things!'

Bill the Lizard's pencil squeaked. Alice could not stand that, so she went round behind him and quietly took it away. The poor little juror searched for it, then tried to write on his slate with his finger. But, of course, it made no mark.

'Herald! Read the accusation!' said the King sternly.

The White Rabbit blew three blasts on his trumpet, unrolled his scroll and read:

'The Queen of Hearts, she made some tarts,
All on a summer's day.
The Knave of Hearts, he stole those tarts,
And took them clean away.'

'Consider your verdict!' cried the King.

'Not yet, your Majesty!' the White Rabbit hastily interrupted. 'The trial comes first!'

'Call the first witness!' said the King.

This was the Mad Hatter. He had a teacup in one hand and a piece of bread and butter in the other.

'You ought to have finished your tea by now,' said the King. 'When did you begin?'

'Fourteenth of March, I think,' said the Hatter.

'Fifteenth,' said the March Hare, who was also in the courtroom.

'Sixteenth,' said the Dormouse, who was sitting next to Alice.

'Write that down,' said the King. The jury eagerly wrote it down and added it up.

'Give your evidence and don't be nervous,' said the King, 'or I'll have you executed on the spot!'

While the Hatter was giving his evidence, the Dormouse complained to Alice, 'I wish you wouldn't squeeze me so!'

'I can't help it,' said Alice. 'I'm growing!'

'Then grow somewhere else,' grumbled the Dormouse. 'You've no right to grow here!'

'Call the next witness!' said the King.

The White Rabbit, in his shrill little voice, read out the name 'ALICE!'

CHAPTER TEN

Alice's Evidence

'HERE!' CRIED ALICE. She jumped up, forgetting how large she had grown, and knocked over the jury box. The jurors went sprawling into the crowd. Alice picked them up and put them back into the box.

'We cannot proceed till all the jury are in their proper places!' said the King severely.

Alice saw that Bill the Lizard was

upside down, so she put him back the right way up.

'What do you know about this business?' asked the King.

'Nothing!' said Alice.

'That's very important!' said the King.

'Unimportant, your Majesty means,' said the White Rabbit anxiously. Some of the jury wrote down 'Important', some wrote 'Unimportant', and some wrote both.

Then the King read out, 'Rule Forty-two – all persons more than a mile high to leave the court.' Everyone looked at Alice.

'That's not a regular rule!' protested Alice. 'You've just invented it!'

'It's the oldest rule in the book!' said the King.

'Then it ought to be Number One!' said Alice.

'Consider your verdict,' said the King.

'No!' exclaimed the Queen. 'Sentence first, verdict after!'

'Stuff and nonsense!' cried Alice loudly. 'The idea of having the sentence first!'

'Hold your tongue!' bellowed the Queen.

'I won't!' said Alice.

'OFF WITH HER HEAD!' the Queen shouted at the top of her voice.

'Who cares for you?' said Alice. (She had grown to her full size by this time.) 'You're nothing but a pack of cards!'

At this, the whole pack rose up in the air and came flying down on her. Alice gave a little scream, half of fright and half of anger, and tried to beat them off.

All at once she found herself lying on the grassy bank. Her sister was gently brushing away some of the dead leaves that had fluttered down from the tree on to Alice's face.

'Wake up, Alice dear!' she said. 'What a long sleep you've had!'

Collect more fantastic
LADYBIRD 🐞 CLASSICS

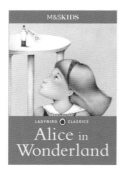

Alice in
Wonderland

Oliver
Twist

Treasure
Island

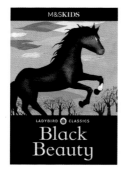

Black
Beauty

Peter
Pan

The Secret
Garden